Buster

the Very Shy Dog
in the
Great Bone Game

by **Lisze Bechtold**

Green Light Readers
HOUGHTON MIFFLIN HARCOURT
Boston New York

Dedicated to my dear friends of Camp Hayashi:
Naomi, Nancy, Mary Ann, Marla, Laura, and Anita

The text of this book is set in 17-point Goudy.
The illustrations are ink and watercolor on paper.

The Library of Congress has cataloged the hardcover edition of
Buster & Phoebe: The Great Bone Game as follows:
Bechtold, Lisze.
Buster & Phoebe: the great bone game/written and illustrated by Lisze Bechtold.
p. cm.
Summary: A clever dog named Phoebe teaches a new puppy, Buster, the value of bones and how to train them.
ISBN: 978-0-618-20862-3 hardcover
[1. Dogs—Fiction. 2. Bones—Fiction.] I. Title: Buster and Phoebe.
II. Titles.
PZ7.B380765 Bs 2003
[E]—dc21   2002151174

ISBN: 978-0-544-66846-1 GLR paperback
ISBN: 978-0-544-66847-8 GLR paper over board

Manufactured in China
SCP 10 9 8 7 6 5 4 3 2 1
4500582930

CONTENTS

Bone Training

Before Buster came to Roger's house,
Bones were something for Phoebe to chew on.

After Buster came, bones were
something for Phoebe to collect.

One day Buster asked Phoebe,
"How did you get so many bones?"
"I saved them up," she answered.
"It makes me feel rich."

"What is *rich?*" asked Buster.
"Rich is when you have lots of bones,"
answered Phoebe, between chews.
"How can you save them if you chew them?"
Buster asked.
"I chew slowly," answered Phoebe.

Suddenly Phoebe looked up.
She dropped her bone and ran outside, barking.

Buster dropped his bone and followed her.

When Buster came back,
His bone was gone.
"Why are your bones
still here and mine isn't?" he asked.

"My bones are well trained, like me," said Phoebe.
"You are just a puppy.
You have a puppy bone.
It is not well trained."
"Oh," said Buster.
He began to chew on the rug.

"Don't chew on that!" cried Roger.
"Chew these."
He gave Buster more bones.
Wow! thought Buster. *I'm getting rich.*

Buster and Phoebe chewed their bones.
Suddenly, Phoebe ran outside, barking.
This time, Buster did not follow her.

Phoebe came back.
"Why didn't you help me guard the house?"
she asked.

"I don't think I should leave my bones alone
until they are well trained," said Buster.
"Oh," said Phoebe. "Would you like me to
help you train them?"

"Okay," said Buster. "Let's train them to stay."
"Okay," said Phoebe. "First, tell them
to *stay* in a very firm voice.
Then run outside and come back."

"Stay!" barked Buster.
He ran outside and came back.

"One of the bones is gone!" cried Buster.
"It was not a smart bone," said Phoebe.
"The smart bones will stay. Try again."
"STAY!" barked Buster.
He ran outside and came back.

Another bone was gone.
"STAY, STAY, STAY!" barked Buster.

He ran outside.
When he came back,
There was only one bone left.

Roger came over to watch.

I hope this is a smart bone, thought Buster.

"STAAAAAAAY!" he growled, and ran outside.

When Buster came back, the bone was still there.

"Hurray!" cried Buster.
"That is one smart bone," said Phoebe.
"Now let's train your bone to sit."

"Maybe later," said Buster.
"I need to chew this one for a while."

The Great Bone

One day, when Buster was all grown up,
an amazing smell came over the fence.
"Wow!" barked Buster.
"Yummy," barked Phoebe.
In the next yard was an enormous dog
chewing an enormous bone.

"I want that bone," whispered Phoebe.

"But, Phoebe!" said Buster, following her.
"It's not your bone. It's *his* bone.
Besides, you already have lots of bones."

"I don't have a bone like that one," said Phoebe.
"Go make friends with him."
She shoved Buster through the fence.

"Um, hi," said Buster.

"Grrrrrrrrrr," said the enormous dog.

Drool slid down his shiny white teeth.

Buster tried to push back through the fence,
but the loose board was stuck.
Buster gulped.
"Um, I'm Buster. What's your name?"
"Grrrrregorrrrry," growled the dog.

"Oh. That's a nice bone you have, Gregory.
Is it trained yet?" asked Buster.
"Huh?" Gregory cocked his head.
"Does your bone know how to stay?"
asked Buster.
"My bone does not know anything,"
said Gregory. "It's a bone."
"It took a long time to train my bones,"
said Buster. "I can help you train yours."
"Really?" said Gregory. "How?"

"Just tell your bone to stay," said Buster.
"Then go away and come back
to see if it listened."
"Okay." Gregory told his bone,
"Stay! Grrrr. STAY!"

25

Gregory ran to the end of the yard and back.

"Wow, your bone stayed on the very first try. I wish my bones had been that smart," said Buster.

"Now let's both go," said Gregory, "to really test it." They ran all the way around the house.

26

When they came back, the bone was gone.

They looked for it all around the yard.

"There it is!" cried Gregory.
"Hurray!" said Buster. "Phoebe found your bone."
"She did?" said Gregory.

Phoebe dropped the bone.
"Some smart bone," she said, licking her lips.

"My friend Buster helped me train it,"
said Gregory.
Buster wagged his tail.
"Phoebe! Buster!" Roger was calling them
in for supper.
"See you later, Gregory," said Buster.

Buster and Phoebe squeezed back
through the fence.
"I still have more bones than you," said Phoebe.
"That's okay," said Buster. "I have a new friend."
And he felt just as rich as Phoebe.

30